Eloise's New Bonnet

STORY BY **Lisa McClatchy**

ILLUSTRATED BY **Tammie Lyon**

Aladdin Paperbacks

NEW YORK · LONDON · TORONTO · SYDNEY

ALADDIN PAPERBACKS

An imprint of Simon & Schuster Children's Publishing Division

1230 Avenue of the Americas, New York, NY 10020

The text of this book was set in Century Old Style.

Manufactured in the United States of America

First Aladdin Paperbacks edition January 2007

4 6 8 10 9 7 5

Library of Congress Cataloging-in-Publication Data

McClatchy, Lisa.

Eloise's new bonnet / story by Lisa McClatchy ; illustrated by Tammie Lyon.—1st
Aladdin Paperbacks ed.

p. cm.—(Kay Thompson's Eloise) (Ready-to-read)

"Artwork in the style of Hilary Knight"—T.p. verso.

Summary: Eloise tries on various hats until Nanny gives her the perfect one.

ISBN-13: 978-0-689-87452-9

ISBN-10: 0-689-87452-9

[1. Hats—Fiction. 2. Plaza Hotel (New York, N.Y.)—Fiction. 3. Hotels, motels,
etc.—Fiction. 4. New York (N.Y.)—Fiction.] I. Lyon, Tammie, ill. II. Thompson, Kay,
1911– III. Title. IV. Series. V. Series: Ready-to-read.

PZ7.M47841375Elo 2007

[E]—dc22

2006012228

I am Eloise.
I am six.
I live in The Plaza hotel
on the tippy-top floor.

I have a dog.
His name is Weenie.

Here is what I like to do:
put sunglasses on Weenie.

Today the sun is shining.
Spring has sprung.
I put my sunglasses on too.

Nanny says, "Eloise,
you need a new hat."

Lampshades make
very good hats.

"No, no, no, Eloise,"
Nanny says.
"You need to find
a real hat."

"I know where to find
a real hat," I say.
"I will visit the kitchen."

Chef's hat makes
a very good hat.

"I know," I say. "I
    will visit room service."

Room service hats
make very good hats.

"No, no, no, Eloise,"
Nanny says.
"That hat has no brim."

"Hmm," I say.
"I will visit
   the bell captain!"

Bell captain hats
make very good hats.

I visit the lobby.
There are hats everywhere!

I try on a lady's hat.
It is a pretty color,
and it has a bird on top.
"Perfect," I say.

Nanny and the manager
do not agree.

KAY THOMPSON'S **ELOISE**

Eloise's New Bonnet

TO PARENTS AND TEACHERS:

Children learn to read in a variety of ways: through formal teaching in school, being read aloud to at home, and reading on their own, using all the tools they've learned for making sense of letters and words. The process starts with a child's first awareness that letters on the page form words, which make sentences, which make stories. No one method of learning is right for every child, but *all* children need books they can read successfully.

Ready-to-Read books feature classic stories and interesting nonfiction by authors who really know how to write for this age group. They're grouped at four levels: Pre-Level One, with repetitive text and simple sentences for children who can recognize words; Level One, with an increased vocabulary and longer sentences for children who are just starting to read; Level Two, for those who are reading independently and are ready for slightly greater challenges; and Level Three, for children who can read fiction and nonfiction on their own, with fewer illustrations and longer texts. At each level, the books are all written, designed, and illustrated to suit the interests, needs, and abilities of new readers.

Children in preschool and the early elementary grades are universally fascinated with reading, and are already saying, "I'm ready to read." When they finish a **Ready-to-Read** book, we want them to say, "I *am* reading, and I like it!"

"Please give the lady
her hat back,"
Nanny says.

"Sorry."

"Eloise, I have a surprise,"
Nanny says.
She hands me a box.

Inside is a new hat
just for me.

Oh, I love, love, love hats!